CASSIE MINT

Santa Baby

BLACK CHERRY
PUBLISHING

First published by Black Cherry Publishing 2021

Copyright © 2021 by Cassie Mint

Cassie Mint asserts the moral right to be identified as the author of this work.

First edition

ISBN: 978-1-914242-51-9

This book was professionally typeset on Reedsy.
Find out more at reedsy.com

Contents

Keep in touch with Cassie!

Want to stay up to date with new releases, sales, and more instalove goodness?

Sign up for Cassie's newsletter!

One

Clara

The front door opens in a swirl of snowflakes, three locals stamping their boots before they enter the bar. I wave at the new-comers from behind the pump, pulling a dark, glossy ale into a pint glass. The bar is crammed, like always, each booth and table and scrap of floor space packed tight with laughing bodies. A fire flickers in the grate on one wall, and the sound of carols mingles with the hubbub of conversation.

It's always busy at Jack's, but tonight is Christmas Eve. Every grown adult in the town has made the pilgrimage here, to laugh and drink and be merry before the marathon that is Christmas day.

And tomorrow morning, the town's parents will nurse throbbing hangovers, questioning their wisdom as their kids squeal and tear open gift paper. The holidays are a wonderful thing.

"Watch yourself."

My best friend Gina bumps me with her hip. Gina's worked behind this bar for almost ten years—way longer than I have—and she's still looking out for me, even when I should know better by now. Her long dark hair tumbles over her generous curves, and her kohl-lined eyes stare pointedly at my hands.

I jolt, slamming the pump off a split second before the glass overflows.

"Thanks," I mumble as I hand the ale over and take the man's money. "Jack would kill me if I spilled beer everywhere again."

Gina snorts, tugging the dishwasher open. "No, he wouldn't."

No, he wouldn't.

Jack may own this bar, may pay all our wages, may be my freaking *landlord* on top of all that—but our boss is no tyrant. If anything, he's too forgiving. Kinder than we deserve.

It only makes me want to please him more.

The glasses clink as we unload the dishwasher, moving in swift, practiced movements to restock the shelves below the bar. We've done this dance a thousand times before, and it's soothing to fall into a rhythm. To not speak to customers for a few minutes.

Look, I love the regulars at Jack's. I like meeting new people too. But sometimes, it's exhausting to be *on* for hours at a time. After my longest, busiest shifts, I feel like barricading my door and never speaking to another human being again.

No one except Jack, maybe. I can't imagine ever not wanting *him* around.

"I got Jack a present."

Gina's words bring an ugly pinch to my chest. Jack and Gina are friends. There's no reason to be jealous, and even if there were—what right do I have to that feeling? None. Jack sees me as a worker, nothing more.

"Oh yeah?" I slide the last glass on a shelf and close the dishwasher with a thump. *Be normal, Clara.* "What did you get him?"

Gina grins and tugs a drawer open next to the cash register. Balled up inside is a red Santa's hat, edged with white and finished off with a pom pom.

"Oh my god." I stare down into the drawer. "You *didn't.*" A woman leans over the bar, waving for service, and I go to meet her. Gina's cackles float after me, and I huff a reluctant laugh before greeting the woman. "Hey there! What can I get you?"

A Santa hat. A *Santa hat.* I bite my lip against a smile as I pour the woman's wine. That's pretty cheeky, even with a super sweet boss like Jack. I can see where Gina's coming from—Jack is burly and bearded. There's silver threaded through his hair, and there's something all-knowing about him too. He *always* knows when we've been bad.

But Santa in the stories is a jolly, grandfatherly figure. And Jack is...

Well. There's nothing *grandfatherly* about our boss. Not with his motorbike and his piercing blue eyes, or the tattoos that wrap around both arms.

But here's my secret: I'd give anything to sit on Jack's knee.

* * *

It was the usual story. Cliched, but no less sad for being that way. My mom's new boyfriend, getting handsy with her teenage

3

daughter. Me telling my mom, and her choosing the new guy over me.

A tale as old as time, I guess. I'm lucky I was seventeen, really. I knew enough about the world to get myself out of there. To take a cross country bus to a brand new town on the edge of a big wood, and to hit the pavement, looking for work and a room.

I tried everywhere. The grocery store and the pharmacy. The library and the nursing home. Nowhere had jobs going—or if they did, they didn't fancy hiring a scruffy runaway to fill the role. Can't blame them, really.

Jack's Bar was the last place on my list. I mean, it was a *bar.* If I weren't desperate, I wouldn't even bother asking, but the sun was sinking in the sky and a cold night was drawing in, and that wood on the edge of town was looking way less friendly than in the daylight.

Jack took one look at my threadbare clothes, soaked through from the rain, and the half-empty duffel bag sagging on my shoulder, and he hired me on the spot. He even let me rent the room above the bar for peanuts, handing over the key right there at my 'interview'.

Interview. Ha. If I'd knocked over every chair in this bar, he'd still have hired me. Jack's wonderful like that.

He didn't ask me tons of questions. Didn't look at me funny, like my mom's boyfriend did, although even back then I probably wouldn't have minded. Jack had less silver in his hair, but he was still a silver fox. All hard muscles and burly shoulders; strong hands and a strong jaw to match.

But my teenage crush went unnoticed. Didn't even register. And Jack didn't let me work behind the bar until I was old enough to drink the booze myself. Until then, I spent almost four years cleaning the booths and collecting empties; helping with filing in Jack's office and placing orders for supplies.

It was good of him to find me work like that. Itty bitty tasks to justify paying my wage. But when I finally got behind that bar... that was such a great day.

I figured he must see me as an adult at last. A grown woman, not a child in need of saving. Twenty one years old—someone he might look at twice. Someone he might look at *closely*.

No such luck. Not so far, anyway.

"You're really going to give him that hat?"

I stand shoulder to shoulder with Gina, scrubbing down the bar during a brief lull. The hours are wearing on, but there's no sign in the crowd waning. New people squeeze through the door every ten minutes, and the roar of conversation builds louder and louder, nearly drowning out the carols.

In the far corner, someone stumbles into the tree, the string lights jiggling, and I wince. It's a scraggly little Christmas tree that I saved up for and bought with my own money—another attempt at saying *thank you* to Jack, for everything.

I'll be thanking that man my whole life and it won't be enough. And that sad little tree... I don't know what I was thinking. Jack hasn't even noticed. But I still wish the customers would be a bit more careful.

"Why not?" Gina nudges me, and it's like she's reading my mind. "You bought him a Christmas tree. We're on theme."

"But Jack will think you're teasing him. Calling *him* Santa."

Gina barks a laugh. "Well, I am."

God. There's no use arguing. When Gina gets an idea, it's full steam ahead. And I love that about her, love her humor and drive, but part of me still squirms at the thought of this gift.

I don't want her calling Jack old. Not even as a joke.

Because what if he listens to her? Then he'll *never* look at me that way.

* * *

I know the exact moment that Jack steps out of his office. I'm sure to everyone else, nothing has changed, but to me—it's like the air shifts. Electricity crackles, and the roar of the crowd fades away, and it's just me and him and my quick, shallow breaths. He surveys the room, hands tucked in his faded jeans and a black long-sleeved shirt clinging to his broad chest, and then he looks over. Our eyes meet.

I grip the edge of the bar so tight the wood creaks.

"Gina. Clara." Jack smiles at us both as he squeezes behind the bar. It's a tight fit back here—barely enough room to open the dishwasher—and Jack's a big man. Tall and broad and so freaking *sturdy*. "How's it going tonight? You two need another pair of hands?"

"We've got it," I say quickly, before Gina can pipe up. Much as I love any excuse to be near Jack, it's Christmas Eve. He shouldn't have to work, not if we can help it. A man like him deserves to have his feet up in front of a fire—or to be drinking freshly-poured drinks at a table with his friends from the town. And if my lizard brain is screaming at me, begging for any excuse for our bodies to brush together as we squeeze past behind the bar... that's my problem, not his.

Jack's eyes land on me again, and·is that a flash of disappointment? Whatever it is, he covers it quickly, nodding and rapping on the bar. "I'll leave you to it, then."

My heart sinks. He's not—not looking at me properly. Jack empties the cash register, avoiding my eye, and I've got this sickly, swooping feeling. Like I've missed a step on the stairs. Like I've misread something *important*.

"Wait, Jack."

I could kiss Gina for keeping him here a while longer. But then she reaches past me, grinning, and tugs open the drawer with his gift. He peers down into the drawer, and when he realizes what he's seeing, his eyebrows shoot up his forehead.

"Santa, huh?"

"Made me think of you." Gina's smile is sly.

Jack laughs, but there's a strain to it. Can't she hear it? Am I the only person paying attention to this perfect man? I grab a cloth and scrub aimlessly at the bar, working my frustration out on the wood.

"What do you think, Clara?" My best friend elbows me. "Want to sit on Jack's knee and tell him you've been good?"

My mouth goes dry. I stop scrubbing, still squeezing the cloth tight, eyes fixed on the bar. *Answer, you idiot.* "I, um. I…"

In the time it takes me to stumble over my words, I go from pale to bright, glowing crimson. The blush spreading hot over my cheeks—it's damning. It tells the whole freaking world that *yes*, that's exactly what I've been picturing. What I've been yearning for in the dead of night.

Gina's grin falters. She was joking, but I forgot to play along.

"Sure," I say weakly, way too late. "That'd be funny."

Funny. The way I feel about my boss is a literal joke. Kill me now. And when I gather up the courage to look at Jack, he's staring like he's never seen me before.

"See." Gina snatches the red hat from the drawer and jams it on Jack's head. She's flustered, trying to cover for me, but we're fooling no one. "Santa. Told you it suits you."

Jack starts to say something, his reply a low murmur, but a customer waves from the other end of the bar and I stumble over, light-headed with relief. I serve the man in a daze, my hands clumsy and my lips numb, and I don't look at my boss and best friend again. Not even once.

For hours and hours, I serve an endless line of customers, and I do it with dry, unblinking eyes and a blush seared into my cheeks. After a while, Gina comes to check on me, her words a soothing murmur.

"You okay, honey?"

I nod, still speechless with horror, loading the dishwasher with dirty glasses.

Gina hums, and the sound is miserable. "I didn't know, Clara, I swear. I wasn't out to cause you trouble."

It's obvious, then, how I feel about Jack. Exactly as I feared.

It takes a few seconds, but I force a reply through my tight throat. "It's okay. It doesn't matter."

But it *does.* It does to me, anyway. Jack's good opinion is the only one I really care about. And he's done so much for me, and how do I repay him?

By pining after him. Making a scene.

I'm so embarrassed. So ashamed.

When the bar closes and the last singing customer spills out into the night, we clear up in record time. Gina and I whirl around the bar like demons are chasing us, wiping down tables and stacking chairs, rounding up glasses and restocking the shelves. Five minutes in, Jack comes out of his office again and leans on the doorway, watching us work. He doesn't offer to join in this time, and we don't ask.

His gaze is heavy on me. My cheeks flush brighter, and I blink back tears.

Jack's office door closes with a snap.

"It'll be okay," Gina tells me, hugging me tight at the end of our shift. We're standing in the doorway, snowflakes swirling in the moonlight, and I'm so tired I'm swaying on my feet. "He'll have forgotten it all by morning."

I nod, miserable, her dark hair tickling my nose. "Can you forget too, please?"

She squeezes me tighter. "Sure, honey. If that's what you want."

When the door closes, I'm left alone in the bar. It's silent, no sound except for the *pop* of the dying embers in the grate and the echoes of earlier conversations still bouncing off the walls.

Golden light glows around the edges of Jack's office door. I pause on my way past, fist raised, but I don't knock. I can't.

My hand drops to my side and I hurry past on silent feet. My heart aches in my chest, long after I've raced up the stairs to my room.

Two

Santa hat. A *Santa hat.* Am I that fucking old already? Maybe I'm reading too much into this. Gina's a sweet girl; she probably meant to poke fun at my beard. And my habit of bringing the workers gifts of hot drinks and cookies during long, cold winter shifts.

And yes, okay, the fact that I'm graying at the temples. And in the beard. And in the chest hair.

I slump back in my desk chair with a groan.

Fuck. I'm a dirty old man.

Because there's a chance Gina meant it as a friendly warning… about Clara. There's no way Gina hasn't noticed the way I look at the young bartender sometimes, when it's been a long day and a headache squeezes my skull and my restraint wears as thin as the frost lacing the windows.

She's so damn beautiful, her caramel hair always braided over one shoulder, stray tendrils framing her heart shaped

10

face. When she's thinking, her pearly teeth dig into her plump bottom lip. There's a tiny gap between her front teeth, and it's so fucking cute, I could slam my head against the bar.

I know Clara's too young for me. Too sweet, too innocent.

I *know* that.

Or my brain does, anyway. And I'm not an animal. My brain's the part that makes decisions, no matter what my body and my heart cry out for.

And make no mistake: they cry out for Clara. They have for almost a year now, ever since she started working behind the bar and I noticed the way the regulars looked at her. Like those men would rather drink *her* down than a pint of beer. Like they were two steps away from crawling onto their bar stools and lunging for her, calling out her name.

Those first few times I noticed, it took every ounce of my self control not to throw those horn dogs out on their ears, marching them bodily across the bar floor. But they never did more than make eyes at her, and unless they cross a line, unless she tells me she's uncomfortable, it's none of my business.

None of my business.

Fuck.

I'd give anything for Clara to be my business. Not as an employee or a tenant, but as a woman. As *my* woman, mine to care for and spoil. Mine to protect. *Mine.*

I've never been the jealous type before. But with Clara...

I don't recognize myself.

"You leave her alone," I mutter to myself—the same thing I tell myself every night when the bar's closed up and we're the only two left in the building. Clara doesn't know I used to crash in the room above the bar before she moved in, and now after late shifts, I can either get a stiff neck on the sofa in my office, or take my bike across town on dark, slippery roads.

She'll never know. She'd worry herself sick with guilt, and there's no need. I'd give her that room a thousand times over. Even if it means putting myself out. Even if it means she's *there* all the time, making me sick with longing.

My chair creaks loudly as I push to my feet, staring around my office with tired, dry eyes. It's dim, lit only by a table lamp, with a woven rug spread over the floorboards and a squashy red sofa pushed against one wall. The painting on the wall is a local artist's, one of the nearby creek, and the bookshelves are crammed with fishing guides and mystery novels instead of the business books I *should* read.

What would Clara change in this room, if I let her decorate it? Would she make it warmer? More homey? Would she change that painting?

Why did she blush so badly when Gina made that joke about sitting on my lap?

I dig the heel of my palm into my eye. Damn stupid thing to wonder. Clara probably felt sorry for me—probably felt awkward because she knows how much I like her, and she agrees that I'm too old.

Midnight is a distant memory as I move around my office, picking up the day's mess, moonlight slanting through the window and lighting up the snowy street outside. I pile up papers and file them away. I log the workers' hours and pay earned—including a nice fat holiday bonus each. And I pass the Santa hat piled on my desk a couple times before swiping it up, jamming it onto my head in a flash of wry humor.

I keep clearing up, the pom pom swinging around my neck.

It's Christmas Eve, after all. And only the worst kind of man can't laugh at himself.

Jack

* * *

The bar is dim when I lock up my office, lit only by shafts of moonlight and the sparkling string lights draped on Clara's tree. She thinks I didn't notice her dragging that sorry little shrub inside a few days ago, but the truth is, I got a lump in my throat when I saw it.

I didn't want to make a big deal. Didn't want to make her uncomfortable.

But these little touches she leaves around the place… they make my heart twist. Make my skin prickle with heat.

Clara got half the picture right: she brought in a fir tree, with fresh, wintry needles, and she wound glowing gold lights through its branches. It cheers up the corner of the bar, warms a spot that would be nothing but shadows otherwise.

But there's one thing missing. At the base of the tree, the floorboards are empty. There are no piles of gifts, no brightly wrapped presents. It's naked. Sad.

Hey, I don't mean Clara should've bought things for *me*. Fuck that. She works hard, and she should keep her money. But it's part of the image, right? Part of the reason for having a tree. And a girl like Clara deserves huge mounds of gifts, endless piles of perfectly wrapped boxes tied with ribbons.

I don't have endless piles of gifts, and my wrapping skills are shitty. But I figured a few bags' worth wouldn't hurt. Wouldn't cross *too* many lines.

Yeah, right. Who am I kidding here?

But I want her to have them. So maybe I just won't tell her it was me.

The shopping bags rustle by my legs as I cross the bar floor, not bothering to flick on a light. There's enough moonlight to see by, and anyhow, this feels like a deed that should stay in the darkness.

Anonymous. Deniable. *Shameful*.

An older man, keeping his messed up feelings in the shadows.

I sigh and kneel before the tree, bags pooling at my sides, and a chill seeps through my jeans. I wrapped these gifts days ago, weeks ago some of them, but as I lift them out one by one, I can picture them perfectly beneath my shoddy wrapping.

A box of those fancy teas that Clara likes—the ones she hoards like a squirrel, only allowing herself one cup a week.

A vanilla-scented candle for her attic room.

A cross-stitch kit.

A novelty shot glass with her favorite cartoon character.

A soft, pale green scarf to replace the one she snagged on a bramble last month in the woods. It's not an exact match to the one she lost, but the shade will go just right with her eyes.

On and on they go, small gifts and trinkets that all together tell a damning truth—that I've been watching her. Obsessing, even. Remembering every tiny detail, storing tidbits away like a dragon sprawled on a pile of gold.

If Gina didn't think badly of me before tonight, she will now, and yet I can't bring myself to stuff the gifts back in the shopping bags. Not when I know they'll make Clara smile.

"Ho fucking ho," I mutter under my breath, the Santa hat pom pom sliding against my shoulder as I work. The last gift crinkles in my grip as I place it beneath the tree: the latest book by Clara's favorite author. Something sexy with werewolves in it. Best not to wonder too much about that one.

A floorboard creaks behind me, and I freeze, kneeling beside the branches. String lights twinkle an inch from my nose, and my heart sinks all the way to the base of my belly.

Busted.

I know those quiet footsteps; that faint coconut scent. That hitch in her breath haunts my dreams.

I'm caught, and there's no getting out of this. There's only one person that could be.

Three

Clara

I can't sleep. Almost an hour of laying in bed, staring at my attic ceiling, and I'm still horrified. Radioactive with embarrassment. Every time I huff out a breath or roll over, trying to get drowsy, my chest twinges with the memory of Gina's jokey question.

What do you think, Clara? Want to sit on Jack's knee and tell him you've been good?

My cheeks still burn hot enough to fry an egg.

The look on Jack's face. His *stare.*

I need to leave. There's nothing else for it. He knows how badly I want him now, and that will only make things awkward. Will only ruin everything good that we have. I've probably outstayed my welcome anyhow, and the right thing to do, the *grateful* thing, is to look for new work. Not to take advantage of Jack's caring nature any longer.

My eyes are raw from crying when I roll out of bed in a chorus of springs, jamming my cold feet into my slipper boots. I slide a red wool sweater over my pajama shirt, shivering in the chill.

Part of the reason Jack barely charges me at all for my room is because it's just that: a single room. If I need the bathroom, I use the one by his office. There's a shower in there, too. And Jack bought me a hot plate and a mini fridge, but if I want a glass of water, I have to come down to the bar.

I try not to come down in my pajamas. It's creepy when I'm the only one here and Jack's finally gone. But crying makes my throat raw, and if I lay in that bed feeling sorry for myself another minute, I'll go mad.

So. Water it is.

The steps are old and wooden, prone to creaking underfoot, so I'm careful to place my feet on the sturdier edges. This is a habit from when Jack's working late and I don't want to disturb him, but I keep it up when I'm the only one here.

Like I said, the bar's creepy late at night. I don't want to draw any attention.

My sweater sleeves hang over my hands, only my fingertips bared to the night air. I run one palm along the banister as I climb down, and the only sound is the whisper of wool over polished wood. Below me, the bar is dark and empty, the lights on my tree flickering in one corner.

I freeze, one foot on the bar floor.

Something shifts beneath the tree.

Oh my god. I wet my lip, checking Jack's office, but it's locked up with the lights out. My heart hammers at my rib cage, my muscles bunching under all my layers. I'm alone here. Vulnerable. Would the neighbors hear if I yelled? I—

"Hey, Clara." Jack's voice is quiet. Resigned. "Couldn't sleep?"

I melt back against the banister, so relieved my head spins.

"Jack. Thank god. I thought you were… I don't know." I choke out a laugh. "Someone scary."

He laughs quietly too and pushes to his feet. The tree lights wash over him as he stands, and I snort.

"The Santa hat again, huh?"

"Yeah, you got me. I think it's my color." Jack brushes his hands against his jeans, and I pause. Squint harder into the darkness.

"What were you doing over there?"

Because there's nothing there but the tree. The scruffy little tree that I brought here, dragged here all by myself, and that he barely even noticed before.

Jack's sigh cuts through the quiet. He shifts his weight, but doesn't come away from the branches. "Getting into character, I guess."

…Huh?

I don't bother stepping quietly, not now that I know it's him. I hop down fully off the steps and wind between the bar tables, my pajama pants rustling together. Jack is silent as I come closer, and when I spot what he's been doing, I see why.

There are gifts beneath my tree. About a dozen small packages, wrapped in glossy white paper.

My heart pounds harder again, but it's not from fear this time. It's from heartache. Love. *Longing.*

"Jack…"

I should thank him. Tell him he didn't have to do this. Maybe even ask him why he did. But I can't speak, can't do more than stare at the pile of gifts, the flickering lights of the tree shining on the paper.

"You've been good this year," he jokes, trying to fill the silence, but it sounds forced. Awkward.

What do you think, Clara? Want to sit on Jack's knee and tell him you've been good?

Yes. I want that so badly.

Then: "I have," I announce, and it's like someone else has taken over my body. Someone confident. Someone who goes after what she wants. Because I step forward, hands trembling but chin high, and push Jack a few steps back until his legs hit the edge of the nearest booth.

Jack sinks down to sit on the bench, staring up at me.

I hold my breath and nudge his legs wider apart, stepping between them.

Because it has to *mean* something right—the pile of gifts? The way he looks at me sometimes? The way he's so tender with me, so sweet?

Maybe. Maybe not. Maybe he's just a good guy. But if I've decided I'm leaving anyway...

What more is there to lose?

And maybe I'm not bold like Gina, but I've always been brave when it counts. I ran away from my old home. I got myself this job. And now... I can do this, too.

Pulse racing, I perch on Jack's thigh, winding one arm around his broad shoulders. His leg is sturdy beneath me, hard with muscle, and after a pause, a strong arm wraps around my waist, steadying me so I don't topple back.

"What are you doing, Clara?" Jack sounds strained. And when I study him in the flickering lights, his strong jaw is clenched beneath his short silver-threaded beard.

I take a deep breath. Count to five, gathering all my courage. Then blow it out in one go.

"Hey, Santa." I cling to Jack's gray sweater. My heels swing beneath his legs. "You're right. I've been *so* good this year."

* * *

Jack barks out a surprised laugh. He sounds half alarmed, half turned on. Like he can't decide whether this is real, or whether I'm playing a stupid prank, but either way, the arm around my waist hooks me tighter against him. My shoulder presses against the hard swell of his barrel chest.

And yeah, it's real. I've freaking *dreamed* of this lap. He smells as good as I thought he would. Like frost and pine and the gingerbread he brought us part way through our shift.

"Have you?" Jack manages, voice tight. "Is that right, Clara?"

"Uh-huh."

"And what gifts do you want, since you've been so good?" Jack winces as he says the words, like he thinks I'm going to turn on him. Get angry at him for playing along.

Um, no. This is better than I'd hoped for.

I point at the pile under the tree. Some of the packages have crimson ribbons tied around them. "I'd like those, please."

I mean, who knows what's in them? But they're from Jack, so I love them already.

"Deal," Jack says, like this is a boardroom negotiation, not a Santa role play. "Anything else?"

Here goes. I grip the pom pom at the end of his Santa hat, squeezing it like a stress ball, and lean in until my breath mists over his neck.

A shudder rolls through him. It's so strong, I wobble in his lap, lunging to cling on tighter, but there's no stopping this now. I'm a runaway train, barreling down the tracks.

"There's one more thing I want," I whisper. My face is so close, his beard tickles my cheek.

"And what's that?" Jack grates out. He sounds wrecked.

I catch his earlobe between my teeth. Bite down gently, then soothe the nip with my tongue. And I finally tell my boss, the man turned to stone beneath me: "I want you, Jack."

Four

Jack

I'm not proud of it, but my first thought is: *she's mocking me.* Why else would a beautiful young woman say she wants a man like me?

But I don't say it out loud, thank god, because this is Clara, and Clara is not cruel. She doesn't toy with people's emotions, and besides—she's flushed. Breathless. Squirming in my lap like she's as worked up as I am.

I clamp one hand down on her thigh. Hold her in place. If she wriggles any more, she's gonna brush up against something she's not ready for.

"You want me?" I need her to say it again. Say it clearer. Spell it out for me, so it gets through the ringing in my head.

"Yes." Clara leans in again, tracing the cold tip of her nose along my cheek, and I screw my eyes shut. The scent of her coconut shampoo is everywhere, invading my senses. Addling my overworked brain.

"You want me like—like that?" I clear my throat. Shit, this is awkward. "Intimately?"

She nods. "Uh-huh."

"Now, wait. Wait a minute." I jiggle her on my knee. Clara squeals and laughs, clutching at my shoulders to hold on, and it's so distracting I can barely force the words out. "Do you want me as Jack? Or as Santa?"

Look, I'm not one to judge. It takes all sorts, and if Clara has some kind of Santa fetish, I won't tease her too badly for it. But I need to know if this is something bigger, if it's the thing I've been dreaming of for a year, or if it's all because I put on this stupid hat.

Would I tell her no, if she only wanted the role play?

Probably not. I'm weak when it comes to Clara.

She snorts, and tugs on my pom pom. "Both. I've never liked Santa that way before, but when it's you..."

Hell yeah. I'll take that answer. And now my chest is swelling, and I'm sitting up straighter, and the string lights seem to glow brighter as I rearrange Clara in my lap, turning her to face forward and bracketing her waist with my hands.

She wants me? She'll get me. I'm done feeling guilty about my feelings. Maybe it looks wrong from the outside, but there's nothing bad about the way I love Clara. I want only good things for her. I want her to be happy. *Satisfied.*

"Tell me." My command is rough. "Tell me how good you've been, baby."

She trembles on my thigh. Lets out a tiny, relieved sigh. Then Clara melts back against my chest, her head resting on my shoulder, and begins to speak.

"I work hard in the bar."

I squeeze her waist in a gentle pulse. "You sure do."

Clara hums and thinks for a second, then adds: "I keep my room tidy."

My thumbs rub back and forth over her ribs. Back and forth. She's wearing a thick wool sweater and her pajamas underneath, but I can still feel the shape of her. She's soft and curvy. Made to fill my big hands. She's *perfect*. "That's good."

"And I…" Clara trails off, but there's no way that's the whole list. I wait patiently, pressing my face against her head so I can smell her hair. Whatever brand shampoo she uses, I need to buy a bottle. Keep it by my bedside, so I can sniff her anytime.

"I'm a good friend to Gina," she says at last. "I listen to her problems. Text her things she'll find funny."

My chest rumbles in approval. My hands trace higher up her sides, until my fingers brush the sides of her breasts. "You're a sweet girl, Clara."

She snorts. "I'm not."

That's bullshit. Anyone who ever met Clara knows she's sweet, but I don't argue. I give her a chance to explain. And while she's chewing over her words, her fingers plucking absentmindedly at my sleeves, I duck my head. Drag my lips along the heated skin of her neck.

Yeah, she blushed like crazy earlier. Blushed so hot, her burning cheeks practically warmed up the whole bar. She's *still* blushing, the red tinge warming her skin.

Guess now I know why. Little Clara was busted. Caught wanting something she thought she shouldn't.

"Oh," Clara mumbles, her head turning to give me better access. I work my way up her throat, pressing hot, whiskery kisses, sucking and nibbling at her soft skin. "I can't—can't think when you do that."

Me neither. My hands slide around her body, palming her soft tits. Weighing them in my palms, squeezing them, *kneading* them, and all the while I keep kissing.

"Jack," Clara breathes. "I can't believe we're doing this."

I pull my head up. Clear my throat, sitting back, but I keep my hands on her tits. Can't help myself.

"You want to stop?" My thumbs find her hard nipples, even through her layers. As I pinch, she sucks in a sharp breath, wriggling against my leg.

"*No.* Oh my god. Don't you dare."

"Then tell me something, Clara." Our voices are soft in the empty bar.

"Tell you what?"

I press my words against her soft hair. "Tell me why you don't think you're sweet."

Clara falls silent. Slumps back against my chest again. Then admits in a low voice: "Some of the things I think about aren't sweet. Some—some of the things I *do*—"

She cuts off, embarrassed.

I've never wanted to hear the end of a sentence more.

"Tell Santa all about it." Maybe if I keep this light, keep it playful, she'll spill the beans. And sure enough, Clara hiccups a laugh. Shakes her head.

"If Santa knew about this stuff, he'd fall off his sleigh."

"Try me," I growl. I'm not some jolly old saint from the North Pole. I've thought plenty of less-than-sweet things about Clara. Things that would make her eyes go wide.

Plenty of nights, knowing she's asleep just upstairs, I've gripped my cock in my office. Worked myself over, thinking about climbing those steps and joining her in that single bed. Pushing her pretty legs apart and wedging myself home.

I've never said a word, obviously. Thoughts aren't actions, after all, and I was sure I'd scare her. Make her feel awkward in her home.

But now...

"Have you touched yourself, Clara?"

She splutters, clutching my sleeves. "How... how did you *know?*"

Fucking hell. "Did you touch yourself and think of me?"

"I... I..."

Enough dancing around it. "Because I've done that, Clara. I've jerked my cock to the thought of you. To the image of your soft tits and your creamy skin and what's hidden between your legs."

She's frozen. Her breaths are quick and ragged, and fuck, I've gone too far. But when I start to move my hands off her tits, she slaps her palms on top. Holds them in place, whimpering when I curse quietly, squeezing her again, my forehead pressed against the back of her head.

"Yes."

When she finally answers, I've almost forgotten the question. But then I remember, and the image of her doing that slams into me like a brick wall.

"Clara," I grind out, eyes screwed shut, shaking my head. "You're right. You *have* been bad."

Five

Clara

~∾✧∿~

"Hey!" I spin around on Jack's lap, embarrassment forgotten, and pin him with a glare. "Doing—doing that isn't *bad*. It's perfectly natural."

He grins, his beard shifting in the moonlight. "I know, baby. I'm just checking you know, too."

I huff, but okay. He got me. I was never really ashamed of touching myself, only of… what Jack might think. If he knew he starred in my nightly fantasies. If he'd be horrified by it.

But I guess I got that answer too. Because when I spun in his lap, my thigh pressed against the front of jeans, and I felt it. The rock hard length of him, jutting against his fly.

He waits, but I don't move my leg away.

"Clara," Jack warns in his gravelly voice.

I wet my bottom lip. Then squirm a little closer. "Uh-huh?"

My movements draw a groan out of him. Dredge it from somewhere deep in his chest. And then he's moving, lightning fast, scooping me out of his lap and depositing me on the booth table next to him. Jack spins on the bench, Santa hat swinging against his shoulder, and then I'm sprawled in front of him like a meal.

"You like to touch yourself, Clara?" Jack's voice drops lower. "Show me."

And okay, I've even had this exact fantasy, although in my version I was sitting on Jack's desk rather than on a booth table. But in my fantasy, I was confident. Sultry. I knew exactly what to do to drive my boss wild.

The reality is different. I'm bundled in baggy pajama pants and slipper boots; the night air is cold, so cold I wince as I lean back and peel down my waistband.

I settle back on the table, bare ass against chilled wood.

And it hits me then, the chasm between us. How Jack is experienced, and worldly, and mature, and *hot*, and I'm just a clueless girl less than half his age who's never even made herself come.

He wants me to show him, but I barely even know what I'm doing.

I go still on the table, misery pulsing through me in waves.

"Clara?" Jack is alarmed. He leans forward, urges me to sit up straight, then grips my shoulders. "What is it? Did I take things too far?"

I sniffle and shake my head. Jack didn't do anything wrong. But he still looks wrecked as he rubs my collarbone, lifting one hand to tuck my hair behind my ear.

"We can stop. We're stopping right now, okay? Please, baby. Don't cry."

"I'm sorry," I rasp. My throat is so tight, but he deserves an explanation. Because I know what Jack is like, and he'll blame himself for this. Will hate himself, and all because my confidence drained away quicker than it came. "I just... I've never..." I sigh and drop my chin. Stare at the checked navy and white pattern of my pajamas, and confess in a whisper, "I don't really know what I'm doing. It's never worked for me."

Silence.

It stretches on, taut and awkward.

Then Jack jerks his head from side to side, like he's shaking himself awake. "Okay, help me out here. You're upset because you've never come?"

I nod, miserable. "I know you want to watch, but I can't get there, I never have, and I hate disappointing you—"

Jack hushes me, and there's a relieved smile crinkling his eyes. "I'm not disappointed. It wasn't a test, Clara. You don't get extra points if you finish."

I smack his shoulder, but I'm relieved too. An answering smile tugs at my mouth.

Maybe I'm being crazy. Overreacting. Maybe this...

Maybe this doesn't have to end yet.

"Can we keep going?" I blurt. "I feel better now. A lot better. But... maybe we could do something else?"

Jack's watching me closely. He's tempted, but he's not sure. And this might be my only chance with the man I've wanted forever, so I push forward. Say what I'm thinking for once. What I'm hoping for.

I take a deep breath, then put it out there. "Maybe you could do it for me."

* * *

Jack is a statue in the booth. The tree lights pulse and flicker, the glow casting shadows over his face and hollowing his cheeks. With the frosted window behind him, his silhouette is broad shouldered, and when he takes a deep breath, his chest swells and falls under his gray sweater.

"Clara… you were upset a few moments ago."

I scoot to the edge of the table. My pajama bottoms are still tangled around my legs, but it's too late to worry about that now. I shuffle up until my slipper boots dangle against Jack's sides, and I can wind my arms around his neck. His short beard snags against my wool sleeves. I steal a quick kiss—a brush of his lips against mine.

"I know. And we don't have to." I bat his Santa hat pom pom. It swings around to the other shoulder. "But I *do* want to. I promise. I've never wanted anything more."

Jack curses under his breath, and his eyes drop between my legs. Like he's fought it too long, but he can't resist the weight of gravity, drawing his gaze down.

I fight the automatic impulse to close my thighs. I *want* him to see me. To touch me.

Maybe even taste me, like I've read about.

And as I watch, hunger sharpens his gaze. Jack clears his throat, a nerve leaping in his jaw. "You're sure? You want me to touch you, Clara?"

I nod, so fast it makes me dizzy. "I do. I want whatever you'll give me. I want all of it when it comes from you."

It's a raw confession, and I'm saying way too much, laying myself bare, but it doesn't scare him off. If anything, it sharpens his resolve. Jack grips my thighs, squeezing once before running his palms up and down my legs, up and down, and when he gets to the tangle of my pajama pants, he tugs them down to my knees, my calves, my ankles.

"Lie back," he says once he's done. There's a hard set to his jaw.

I bite my lip and obey.

It's a small mercy, I think, when Jack tugs the Santa hat off and tosses it onto the table beside me, the fabric landing with a soft *thump*. This night is going to ruin me enough for all other men—I don't need a visual of Santa Claus licking between my thighs. I'm a therapist's worst nightmare as it is.

"I'm going to make you come, Clara."

I splutter a laugh, grinning at the dark ceiling. "You can sure try."

Jack makes a rumbly noise. Like there's no doubt about it, none at all. "Consider it another Christmas Eve gift."

His hands land on my thighs again, his warm, dry palms against my bare skin.

I shiver. I've always loved gifts.

The table is cool and hard beneath my back, the air in the bar so cold, my breath practically fogs above me in little clouds. I pant and gasp and twitch as Jack nudges my legs wider apart, grips my ass in both hands, and tugs me towards him, burying his face in my bare pussy.

I don't know what I expected. Something slower, maybe, more teasing, more careful, careful like Jack is every damn day, but I guess I've been driving him wilder than I realized. Because the second Jack's restraint snaps, he's hungry, *starving* for me, groaning loudly as he licks a broad stripe up my seam. He works me over until his jaw cracks, his beard tickling my inner thighs, slickness spreading over my pussy, my lower stomach, my legs.

Jack eats me like a man possessed. Like I'm his last meal. No—like I'm the plate of cookies left out for Santa Claus.

And me? I *love* it. I love every lick, every stroke of his hot, broad tongue. I bury my hands in his silver-tinted hair, and I cling on for dear life, grinding my hips up against him.

"Jack! Oh my god. That—that feels—" I break off, panting. I don't have words for how it feels, only strangled moans. It's so much hotter and wetter, so much more *intense* than I could ever have imagined.

"Fuck, baby." His words vibrate against my pussy, tingling in my clit. "You taste so fucking sweet." He licks me again, sucking my folds into his mouth then letting them go with a *smack*. "Like icing sugar."

His hands squeeze my ass cheeks, his grip pulsing around me once, and then he's drawing one hand away. Snaking it between us.

His fingertip prods gently at my entrance. Swirls in tiny circles, gathering wetness. Then Jack's pressing forward, pressing into me up to the first knuckle, and he's lapping at my clit, and I'm pulling his hair. It's all so much and not enough, and moisture brims in my eyes as his chest rumbles, and he slides his finger deeper.

"So fucking tight." He crooks his finger, rubbing at my walls. "We'd have our work cut out for us if you ever wanted my cock."

"I do," I gasp, staring glassy-eyed at the ceiling. My spine bows. "I do. I already want it."

Jack chuckles darkly, then slides his finger all the way in, pumping slowly in and out of me. The friction drives me insane—it's like being tickled, but a million times better.

When his lips close over my clit, I curse loudly at the empty room. And when he crooks his finger inside me, tongue dancing and breath hot…

I shatter.

That's what it feels like. There's no other way to describe it. Like I'm a priceless vase, trembling on the edge of a high shelf, and Jack nudges me forward. Sends me spinning through the air to shatter into a thousand pieces. My shards fly in all directions, and my mind is blank, my blood is racing, and I'm clamping down on his finger like I'm trying to break it off.

A hundred years pass before I float back down to my body. I lie on the table, panting and boneless.

"Told you you'd come."

I kick at Jack's sides, eyes still closed. He laughs, then pulls my pajama pants back up my legs. I lie there like a doll and let him dress me again, putting me right and tugging me to sit up, where he smooths down my hair.

His kiss is so sweet. I part my lips on a sigh, and then our tongues slide together, and I can taste myself in his mouth.

Icing sugar? If he says so. I taste kind of salty to me, but hey—I'm not going to complain if he likes it.

"Come on." Jack kisses my nose, then eases me down off the table. "It's late. Good girls should be asleep."

Six

Jack

I keep a close eye on her, but Clara seems fine. She still smiles at me like I'm her hero in the warm glow of the tree; she stifles a laugh in her sleeve as I grab a spray cleaner and cloth from behind the bar and wipe down the booth table.

"Gotta be responsible." I wink at her, scrubbing.

Clara beams.

So… maybe this is okay. Maybe I haven't done something terrible here. Maybe she wants this as badly as I do.

Maybe it can happen again.

Fuck. I'd give anything for this to happen again. For Clara to touch me casually, to kiss me on the cheek in the mornings, for her to let me back between those butter-soft thighs. And if she'd let me be her man? Forget it. I'd kill for that role.

Clara yawns so wide, her jaw cracks.

"Alright, then." I tuck the cleaning stuff away and steer her toward the staircase. Her slipper boots scuff over the floorboards. "Up we go."

How many times have I thought about climbing these steps to see her in her room? More than once, in the dead of night, I've had the horrible urge to sneak up here and watch her sleep.

I didn't, obviously. I'm not a complete psycho. But my heart pounds as I climb behind her, that curvy little ass swaying in her pajama pants.

"It's nearly morning," Clara mumbles, her words thick with exhaustion.

"You're going to bed anyway."

"Yeah, yeah, I know. But you won't go across town this late, will you?"

The worry in her voice makes my chest glow warm. "No, I won't. I promise. I'll crash in my office for a few hours."

Her voice is small when she replies: "Oh."

Look, I know what she was hoping for there. But I remember, even if she doesn't, that her bed is a cramped single cot. Barely big enough for one person, let alone sweet little Clara plus a whole grown man. We won't fit, not comfortably, and she desperately needs some good sleep.

Clara doesn't speak again as we climb to her room.

I hover awkwardly in the doorway as she settles in. Since I'm not staying, it seems wrong to tramp in there and get in the way. Clara kicks off her slipper boots and throws the bed covers back, lowering down with a crinkle of bed springs.

There's no need for me to be here at all, not really, but I wasn't ready to leave her yet. And some mixed up part of my brain wanted this to be like a date, one where I walk her home.

"Goodnight." Clara flops down on her side, tugging the covers over her shoulder. I smile at the pink tip of her nose, but I can't tell if she smiles back.

"Merry Christmas, Clara."

"Merry Christmas, Jack." Her voice sounds funny. Strained.

My boots thud against the stairs as I retreat to the bar. I'd be a shit Santa Claus in real life—I'm not built to sneak. And no way would I fuck around with chimneys when buildings have perfectly good doors.

I swipe the red hat off the table on my way to my office, twisting it in my hands.

Then close the door with a snap, nerves churning in my gut.

* * *

I toss and turn on my office sofa, my mind racing a thousand miles an hour. The more I stew in the darkness, the more my body joins in, sweat prickling over my top lip and my heart pounding faster. I scrub my hands down my face, restless.

Did I upset Clara when I came back down here?

Maybe I should have just stayed up there. Dragged a chair next to her bed or something. I mean, I'm sure as shit not getting any sleep anyhow, and now my baby's up there doubting me. Feeling abandoned.

Fuck.

I push upright on the sofa, stifling a groan.

Sometimes, I feel young. Fit and sprightly. And sometimes, when I try and sleep on this fucking sofa, I feel like death warmed up. I roll my neck, wincing at the ache, and jam my feet in my boots before pushing to stand.

I'll just check in on her. Nudge the door open and peek through. And if she's already sleeping, I'll leave her be and talk to her about it in the morning.

The floorboards groan under my weight as I cross the small office. Already, the voices of reason clamor in my head, telling me to *turn around, Jack,* and *let that girl alone.* But the thought of Clara feeling sad up there has chased the last shreds of control clean out of me.

I yank the office door open and freeze.

Clara blinks up at me, fist raised. She's still bundled in that red wool sweater, but her hair's loose now, mussed and wavy over her shoulders from being in that braid.

I'm the first to recover. "Clara? You okay, baby?"

The pet name gives her a jolt. And she smiles up at me, sweet but unsure. "Hi, Jack. Um. I know you told me to go to bed, but I was lying up there missing you and I couldn't sleep because of it. Um."

Missing me. She was up there, *missing* me. I rub at the ache in my chest, drawing her into the office by the elbow with my other hand.

"Okay, uh. Well. It's cold in here," I warn her, closing the door again. "And the sofa's not too comfy. But you can stay as long as you like." I flick on a table lamp, the room washing gold.

When I turn back to Clara, the breath catches in my throat. Because that light—it brings out the burnished threads of her caramel hair. It shows the dusting of freckles over her nose, and her pale green eyes, and the cute little gap teeth digging into her bottom lip.

"You take the sofa," I rasp. "I couldn't sleep on it anyway."

"Thank you, Jack." She makes no move toward it. Just stands there, staring up at me, like she's willing me to understand.

Well, hell. I can't read my own mind most days. What chance do I have with Clara?

As we stand there, an awkward silence brewing, the wind kicks up outside. It howls and slams against the window, rattling the glass in the frame, and I swear the temperature drops a few more degrees.

Clara shivers, hugging her waist against the cold.

"Here." I snatch the tartan wool blanket off the back of the sofa, draping it around her slender shoulders. Then I cast around for more layers to offer her, but the only thing I find is that damn Santa hat.

Oh well. A layer's a layer. I swipe it off the desk and ease it onto her head.

Clara's hair is like silk where it brushes my knuckles. The hat's way too big for her, sagging backwards off her head, but it's worth putting it on her for the smile she gives me.

"My turn, huh?"

I chuck her chin. "I guess so." Seriously, I can't stop *touching* her. Any excuse, and my hands are all over her, my pulse ticking faster in response.

Clara turns and flops down on the sofa, grinning up at me. "You want to sit on my knee, Jack?"

"Baby, I'd flatten you."

She nods, pretending to be serious. "Yeah, but I've thought about it. That's how I'd like to go."

Ah, damn it. She's so fucking sweet. And I'd kind of like to flatten her, too, but not by sitting on her knee. I'd like to stretch out on top of her, cover her with my whole body, feel her curvy little frame under mine, and rut her into those sofa cushions until she's a puddle of need.

Clara bites her lip, clutching the blanket tighter around her shoulders. "You're looking at me funny, Jack."

"Am I?"

"Yeah."

I take one step closer. Just one step. It's all I can trust myself with. "Funny how?"

"Funny like earlier." She sucks in a breath, and it's ragged. "Funny like I'm something to eat."

I can't help my chuckle. I take another step, the floorboards groaning. "Well, so you were."

Staring at her the way I am, I see the exact moment twin spots of color start to glow on her cheekbones. Those spots are the starting line, and from there the blush spreads over her cheeks, her nose, and down her pretty throat. I watch its progress, fascinated, and I forget myself for a moment, lowering to sit next to her on the sofa.

"You're flushed, Clara. What are you thinking about?"

She swallows. Shakes her head, not saying anything.

"You won't tell me?"

Clara shrugs one shoulder.

And maybe I should let it go, but she came to *me,* said she was lying awake missing me, and this night is nearly over, the pale tinge of dawn creeping over the windows. It seems to me that if we leave things unsaid now, if we let things stay tangled, it'll be much harder to untangle them in the daylight. And I don't want things messy with Clara. They're so simple, coming from my side.

So I prod her a little. I'm not proud of it.

"Why did you come find me, Clara?"

Her plump mouth twists, her fingers squeezing the tartan blanket. "I told you, Jack. I missed you."

"So this is all you wanted? The two of us, sitting in the same room?"

She shrugs again, and she looks so miserable that I take pity.

Start talking, before I can think better of it.

"You know what I think? I think you wanted me to touch you again. Maybe lick between your legs. To make you come a second time. Is that right?"

Her blush flares brighter, and triumph swells in my chest, but then she's shaking her head again. Well, shit.

I try not to look too much like my chest is caving in. Like cold is spreading through me, icier even than the snow outside. "No? That's okay." My voice is pure gravel. "You can just sleep here if that's all you want. I'll sit at the desk and keep out of your way."

I move to stand up, but Clara grips my sleeve. Holds me in place, her knuckles white against my sweater.

Seven

Clara

He's thinking the worst again. And I can't blame him, really. Jeez, why can't I say what I want? Why can't I be brave and say the words out loud?

Because now Jack's looking like he hates himself again, and it's my fault. Me and my stupid shrugs.

"Don't go," I beg. His mouth flattens in a line, but he stays put.

Okay. Okay, I can do this.

"I did want something when I came downstairs." His arm is warm and hard beneath his sleeve. Bulging with muscle. I shift on the sofa, mouth dry. "I wanted... I wanted..."

Jack pats my knee, but there's nothing hungry in it. "It's okay, Clara. We'll talk tomorrow."

"No, wait—" I yank on his sleeve, rougher than I should, but he was going to get up again. And this feels important. Like it might be my only chance to say this, to get it right.

Jack settles back against the sofa. He turns to me, mouth down-turned and eyes tight, but even now he can't hide the longing there.

He wants me. And I want him too.

I *will* be brave.

"I came down because I didn't want to be apart from you. And because..." I wet my lips, picking my words carefully. "Because I was lying in bed *wanting* you. Wanting *all* of you."

Jack hums, and the sound is rough. He's warming over again, coming back to me, little by little. He knots his fingers together, resting his elbows on his knees.

"There are different ways to take that, Clara. Can you tell me a bit more?"

Oh, god. My face burns brighter, but I rally and push on. His sweater is soft in my clammy grip.

"I want..." My eyes drop to his fly, unbidden. Jack grunts, but doesn't move an inch. "I want you to—to take my... to make me..."

Jeez. There's really no good way to say this, is there?

"You want me to fuck you, Clara?"

I snort and nod. I guess that'll do it. And Jack smiles at me, rueful, before shrugging his big shoulders.

"I'm not a poet, baby. But the way I feel about you—that's poetic, alright."

He turns to face me, but I keep squeezing his sweater. "It's my first time," I blurt out. "And I only want to do this if—if you love me. If it's more than one night."

His forehead wrinkles. "Of course I love you. Don't you know that already?"

But I don't mean *love* as in the way he'd love a good friend and longtime employee. I mean *love* as in...

"Clara," Jack says quietly. "I thought you already knew. I'd marry you tomorrow if you let me."

Huh.

Huh.

"I think the churches will be busy," I mumble, head spinning and chest bright. Because no, I didn't know that, but now that I do...

I swing one leg over Jack's lap. He leans back, surprised, but then his big hands clamp down on my hips and drag me closer.

"We doing this, baby?" His piercing blue eyes stare at me, awed, and I wind my arms around his neck, heart thumping.

"Yeah." I shift closer. Roll my hips. Bite my lip at the hard length I find pressed against his fly. "But you might have to show me how."

* * *

I've thought a million times what sex might be like. And specifically, sex with Jack. Because when you've got the hottest man alive as your boss, why would you picture it with anyone else?

I figured he'd be hungry for me. I've caught him staring enough times to be sure of that. And I figured he'd be tender, because he's *Jack*, and Jack is good and kind and wonderful.

I'm half right. He's both those things, but he's so much more, too. Jack cradles me in his lap like I'm the world's greatest treasure—then shoves my sweater and pajama top up and sucks my nipple hard enough to bruise.

He kisses me hard. Slides his tongue into my mouth, biting,

claiming.

And all the while his hands roam over my sides, so gentle.

Rough and tender. Soft and urgent. I'm tossed around in a storm of my boss's conflicting emotions for me, and it's so perfect. Almost overwhelming. Every touch makes me sigh; every nip heats my blood.

He loves me.

I can't believe it. Since when did a runaway ever get so lucky?

"What are you thinking so hard about?" Jack grinds out as he urges me to stand, tugging my pajama pants down my legs.

I kick them off and climb back onto his lap. "You."

The *clink* of Jack's belt buckle is loud in his office. The dawn's coming faster now, washing the room pale blue, and he secures the blanket tighter around my shoulders.

Ha. As if I could feel cold right now. I've got Jack's warm hands squeezing my waist and trailing down my stomach; I've got this freaking Santa hat, slumping to one side on my head.

Jack notches the head of his cock to my entrance. "We'll go slow, okay? Nice and easy. And if you want to stop, you say."

Not likely. I'm already rocking my hips instinctively, trying to urge him inside. I've got that ticklish feeling down there again, and it only gets worse when Jack starts rubbing at my clit, leaning forward to kiss my neck, his beard soft against my skin.

"Sit down on it, baby."

I sink down an inch. "*Oh.* Oh my god."

"Take your time."

Yeah, no kidding. I've only let in the head of his cock, and already I'm stretching around him. There's a faint burn, but it's not unpleasant. It doesn't hurt, exactly, and when he keeps rubbing my clit…

I bite my lip and sink down deeper.

So this is what it feels like to have someone inside you. Someone hard and throbbing. I wiggle my hips, and I'm rewarded with another inch. On and on we go, Jack kissing my neck, my earlobe, my bottom lip, his thumb rubbing steadily at my clit.

And I sink down deeper and deeper, until he's wedged huge and hot inside me, all the way down until my ass rests against his thighs.

"You're there. You've done it." Jack cups my face and kisses me breathless. "So fucking perfect, Clara."

It's not like Jack is stingy with praise on a normal day, but hearing that while his cock twitches inside me? Heat floods through my veins, and I whimper, rolling my hips.

Yes.

This is—this must be what all the fuss is about. This sensation right here, the huge length of him, so unyielding, sliding in and out of my pussy, dragging over every part of me. My toes curl in the frosty air. My pulse leaps.

"That's it. Fuck." Jack grips my hips again, urging me to roll harder. Take him deeper. Every time his cock rubs against a spot inside me, my eyes practically cross. I cling to his neck, our foreheads pressed together, and our ragged breaths fill the quiet office.

The sofa creaks.

The blanket slips off my shoulders.

"Jesus *Christ*," Jack grits out, and the crack of his palm against my bare ass tears a moan from my throat. We're rocking urgently, the slick sounds of our bodies joining echoing around the room.

It's messy. It's primal.

It's perfect.

This time, when I come, it feels different from earlier. The orgasm Jack gave me with his mouth was sharper, more concentrated.

This time, it's like watching a storm rolling towards us over the hills. Building slowly, coming closer, the rains pounding the grass and my lips part, my sighs lost in the wind. It fills me slower, but the pleasure is deeper, somehow, and it spreads to every nook and cranny of my body. Warms me down to the marrow of my bones.

I tip my head back, hips moving in his lap.

Jack's teeth scrape over my throat, and I fall.

"*Jack.*"

"I'm here."

I cling to his shoulders, body jerking, breath held. And when I finally come back to myself, when I start to move again, dazed and blinking, Jack thrusts his cock deep inside me and fills me with wet heat.

I stay in his lap for a long time. Keep him inside me, even once he's softened. I don't want us to be apart, not yet. And when I finally peel myself off him, sticky and aching, Jack follows me up, tugging on my Santa hat pom pom.

"Come on. I bet we can both fit in the shower."

I scoff. The cubicle is tiny; there's no way. But if Jack wants to try, there's no way I'll tell him no.

Besides. I still haven't seen him properly with his clothes off. I've wanted to for years. And inquiring minds need to *know.*

"What do you have planned for Christmas?" I trail behind him out of the office, stealing a glance at my tree with the small pile of gifts. "Are you playing Santa for anyone else?"

Jack scoffs. "'Course not." He pushes the bathroom door open.

"No one else has been good."

I hide my smile, stepping under his arm onto the tiles.

I know it's wrong to be jealous, but I'm glad. This Santa is *mine*.

Eight

Jack

O *ne year later*

    I step out of my office, head throbbing and mouth dry from another long shift. Christmas Eve is always a killer. Everyone for miles around wants to gather, to have a drink or three, and it's a great earner, but the staff are always dead on their feet by the time we close.

Now, though, the bar's empty. Quiet. A big tree glows in the corner of the room, lights glittering and strung with baubles.

I ease my handfuls of bags out of the doorway, careful not to knock them. I may have gone overboard this year.

The thing is, I love all our regulars, but I don't trust them enough to leave Clara's gifts out where they could get trampled. And we have a tree at home, sure, but we both know full well we're not making the trek back across town this late at night on Christmas Eve. Not with Clara perched on my bike. Not on those icy roads. No way, no how.

Besides, Christmas at the bar is kind of a tradition. So it's this tree I cross to, laden with gifts, a Santa hat crammed on my head.

Gina burst out laughing when she saw me wearing it earlier. But Clara's reaction was the best—the radioactive blush that spread over her pretty cheeks.

"I don't want to know," Gina had declared, throwing up her hands behind the pump.

No, she probably doesn't. Gina talks a big game, but she's protective of Clara. Like a big sister. I can't blame her.

My boots thud against the floorboards, and the gift bags rustle as they brush against table legs. I'm most of the way across the room before I see it: the flurry of movement, underneath the branches.

"Huh." I come to a stop next to the tree, my beard shifting as I grin. "You beat me here."

Clara kneels on the floor, dressed in the set of spare pajamas she keeps upstairs, stacking parcels wrapped in shiny paper under the tree. The swell of her belly presses against the shirt, stretching the checked flannel.

"I told you not to get me anything."

Clara snorts. "Well, I didn't listen."

"No, you didn't." I watch her closely, my chest aching with how much I love her. And we're alone now. Finally alone. "You feeling okay after your shift?"

I've urged her to stop working now that she's pregnant, as soon as she wants, but Clara says she wants to work until she drops.

And I told *her* that had better be a figure of speech, but she just laughed. And damn it, I meant it. Clara's feet would barely touch the floor if I had my way. I'd carry her from room to room, and fetch her snacks and hot drinks, and rub her sore shoulders.

Sure, I do those things anyway. But that hard little bump—it drives me mad. Dials all my protective instincts up to eleven.

"What did you get me, little elf?"

Clara shakes her head, stacking another parcel. "You'll have to wait and see tomorrow."

Whatever it is, I'll love it, though not nearly as much as I love the *other* gift she got me, the one growing inside her. It seems too good to be true, but I keep pinching myself, and she's still pregnant, so. Guess this is happening after all. I must have been good in an earlier life.

"You shouldn't kneel on that cold floor."

"And you shouldn't boss me around."

But there's no heat to her words, and Clara lifts a hand when she's ready. Lets me help her up. And when she turns to me, the lights from the tree shine in her big eyes. "Will you be long down here? I want you to keep me warm."

"I'll be less than ten seconds. Wait for me, and I'll carry you upstairs."

Clara laughs, backing towards the stairs. "I'm pregnant, Jack. Not an invalid."

"Humor me." I bend down and unpack the bags as fast as I can, heaping new piles under the tree. When the first step creaks under her foot, I throw the rest under there in a messy landslide, then chase after her across the bar.

Clara runs upstairs, giggling wildly, and I snatch her halfway up the first flight. Sling her—carefully—over my shoulder.

"I feel like Santa's sack." Her words are muffled in my sweater.

I smack her ass. "You can have Santa's sack any day."

Jack

Her explosion of giggles makes me grin, and I take the rest of the steps two at a time. There's a bed waiting for us—a double bed now, thank god—and I've wanted my wife all night. I need to get her warm, then make her come until her toes curl.

"Merry Christmas, Jack," she mumbles into my sweater.

I nod, wishing it back and meaning it. Because this night does have magic to it—she's the proof of that.

This time last year, I was lonely and sick with longing for her.

Clara's a miracle, alright.

* * *

Thanks for reading Santa Baby!

For more snowy romance, check out the Winter Warmers series—starting with Winter Ward. *I let her stay as a favor to an old friend. But her father doesn't realize... he sent a lamb to the big, bad wolf.*

xxx

Teaser: Winter Ward

"Come along, Bellamy."

My father tugs on my elbow, towing me through the dense crowds of the U-Bahn. The underground train station is packed with bodies, loud and humid, and the rattle and roar of trains sucking through the tunnels is constant. I stumble over someone's dropped jacket, and my father slows with a sigh. "Quicker, please. Felix—Herr Vogel does not like to be kept waiting."

Felix.

My father may address the famous composer by his first name—they were neighbors as young boys, after all. But to the rest of the world, and certainly to me, he is Herr Vogel. Legendary composer and ice-cold family friend.

"Are we late?" I hurry to keep up, my skirt swishing around my thighs. If we *are* late, it's not my fault. I'm not the one who couldn't peel myself off his new wife, kissing and giggling in the kitchen like teenagers.

I don't say that, obviously. It would irritate my father, and besides—I'm happy he's found love again. Even a very demonstrative, nauseating kind of love.

"Not yet," my father snaps, tugging on my elbow again, and I roll my eyes and push after him through the crowd. His blond head is a beacon among dark jackets and jewel-toned scarves. Somewhere through the press of bodies, a busker strums an acoustic guitar, and my father squeezes my elbow in warning.

I know, I know. We can't stop to listen.

Not even if the music calls out to me, tugging on the loose ends of my soul.

For all my father's grumbling, we spill out into the street with plenty of time to spare. The stars wink at us from above, dulled by the city lights but still beautiful, and snowflakes swirl on the breeze and melt on my cheeks.

The crowds are thinner up here above the station, but the streets are still full, with couples wandering arm in arm to dinner dates and flustered parents carrying armloads of shopping bags. Everyone is bundled in winter coats, noses flushed and eyes bright against the cold.

My father checks his watch, distracted, and begins to tow me along again, my suitcase bumping against his calf.

"It has wheels," I tell him, hitching my violin case higher under my arm.

Either he doesn't hear me or he doesn't care. That's fine. It's his pant leg getting scuffed.

Even though I've been to the city hundreds of times in my life, I can't help gaping up at the huge buildings like a tourist. The pale stone stretching high overhead, the huge windows, the ornamental balconies—it all feels like it's from another time. Another world. A grander one, and a more brutal one, too.

I can see why Herr Vogel settled here. It suits him.

Our harried journey ends at the stone steps to an ornate town house, three blocks from the U-Bahn station. The house is tucked between a boutique hotel on one side and a coffee house on the other, the cafe still packed with customers and its windows steamed over, even this late in the evening.

No wonder the city is famous for artists and musicians. Everyone here is too caffeinated to ever sleep.

"We're early." My father drops my elbow, checking his watch and shooting me a rueful smile. I smirk back, shaking out my arm.

"Herr Vogel will be happy."

The smile drops off my father's face, as quickly as it came. He glances around, like Herr Vogel could be listening, hanging in the doorway like an eavesdropping bat. And when it's clear we're alone, he steps closer and speaks in low, urgent tones.

"Don't annoy him, Bellamy. Don't get in the man's way. Understand?"

I wrinkle my nose and shrug. It's not rocket science.

"Felix—Herr Vogel is a busy man," my father presses. There's a snowflake quivering on his mustache. "Busy and important."

I stifle a sigh. "Yes, I know."

"I know you like your music, but don't—don't *pester* him, Bellamy."

"Alright."

"Keep to yourself and work on your studies. Iris and I will be back before the New Year, so if you get lonely before then…"

My father trails off. I raise my eyebrows. "Yes? If I get lonely before then…?"

My suitcase thumps to the stone step. Someone laughs loudly across the street. "If you get lonely, call your mother," my father says with great distaste. "Or go out to a coffee house. Just don't bother Herr Vogel with it. Understand?"

Yes, I think, lifting my suitcase in my free hand and waiting as the doorbell trills. My father is already backing away before the intercom crackles in answer, and by the time the door swings open, my father is at the bottom of the steps, arm raised in farewell.

Herr Vogel nods at him over my head, exchanging a quiet greeting and barely glancing at me before turning back inside.

My father's steps echo down the city street.

Yes. I understand.

* * *

The last time I stepped foot in this house, I must have been ten years old. I remember staring open-mouthed at the high ceilings and glittering chandeliers; remember rocking up onto my toes to try to see the oil paintings lining the walls. As a child, Herr Vogel's townhouse seemed more like a museum than a home—all cold marble and heavy drape curtains, a quiet hush permeating through the halls.

At twenty, I like to think I am harder to intimidate. Less likely to lose my tongue when Herr Vogel speaks to me.

But I still packed a few extra sweaters in my suitcase, ready for the cold composer and his even colder townhouse.

"My housekeeper prepared a guest suite for you."

I follow a set of broad shoulders up the winding staircase, noting the way Herr Vogel's tailored white shirt clings to his body. Is it so very physical, composing music? Where the hell did all those muscles come from? The man is lean with a narrow waist, but even through his shirt, he seems harder than marble. Like he could hop up onto a plinth in one of the alcoves and blend in with the other sculptures.

"That was kind of her."

A pair of light gray eyes glance back at me. "Indeed."

I'm glad Herr Vogel is leading the way rather than walking beside me. It lets me stare at him openly, comparing this man to the figure in my memory. He is as tall as I remembered, towering above me, but his black hair is longer, brushing at his collar, and dusted with silver at the temples. His voice, in the rare instance that he speaks, is low and husky, and his hand is strong where it grips my suitcase handle.

Our fingers brushed when he took it from me. I never noticed hands as a little girl, but as a twenty year old woman...

Herr Vogel has beautiful hands.

"I work long hours." Herr Vogel does not turn his head as he speaks, instead addressing the empty hallway in front of us. Doors slip past on either side, and still we keep walking, steps sinking into the dark green rug. "My work must not be disturbed. Do you understand?"

God, why do these men keep asking me that? Do they truly think it's so complicated? Maybe *I* don't want to be disturbed either.

I purse my lips. "I understand."

"However long you plan to stay here—"

"Three weeks, I believe."

He shrugs one shoulder, as if it doesn't matter. "However long you stay, you have access to the full house. All except for my private quarters, of course, and the music room."

My heart sinks. I clutch my violin case closer. "Of course."

What did I expect? That I'd play endless duets with a famous composer? That he would take an interest in me, *teach* me, even allow me to listen to him working?

Ridiculous. I'm here as a favor to my father, nothing more.

Herr Vogel understands that, even if I tried to forget it. Even if for a foolish moment, I let some excitement slip through.

This is not some musician's vacation.

I'm here because I have nowhere else to go.

* * *

Check out Winter Ward!

xxx

Cassie Mint

About the Author

⁂

Cassie writes outrageous, OTT insta-love with tons of sugar and spice. She loves cookie dough, summer barbecues, and her gorgeous cat Missy.

You can connect with me on:

🌐 https://www.authorcassiemint.com
📘 https://www.facebook.com/cassiemintauthor
🔗 https://www.bookbub.com/authors/cassie-mint
🔗 https://www.amazon.com/~/e/B08VF8BPWG

Subscribe to my newsletter:

✉ https://www.authorcassiemint.com/newsletter